DEREK

the Knitting Dinosaur

For my niece, Lynne, and for David—M.B.

For Sue and Jane—K.A.

This book is available in two editions
Library binding by Carolrhoda Books, Inc.
Soft cover by First Avenue Editions
c/o The Lerner Group
241 First Avenue North
Minneapolis, Minnesota 55401

Text copyright © Mary Blackwood 1987.
Illustrations copyright © Kerry Argent 1987
First published 1987 by Omnibus Books, Adelaide, Australia, in
association with Penguin Books Australia Ltd.

Library of Congress Cataloging-in-Publication Data

Blackwood, Mary.
   (Derek the dinosaur)
   Derek the knitting dinosaur / by Mary Blackwood ; illustrations
by Kerry Argent.
       p.   cm.
   Previously published as: Derek the dinosaur.
   Summary: Derek, a little green dinosaur, is somewhat worried that
he likes to stay home and knit instead of acting like his ferocious
brothers, but the onset of cold weather allows his knitting to
become useful.
   ISBN 0-87614-400-8 (lib. bdg.)
   ISBN 0-87614-540-3 (pbk.)
   [1. Dinosaurs—Fiction. 2. Knitting—Fiction. 3. Brothers—
Fiction. 4. Behavior—Fiction. 5. Stories in rhyme.] I. Argent,
Kerry, 1960-   ill. II. Title.
PZ8.3.B574De   1990
[E]—dc20   89-35734
                                                    CIP
                                                    AC

Manufactured in the United States of America
3 4 5 6 7 8 - P/MP - 01 00 99 98 97 96

DEREK

the Knitting Dinosaur

by Mary Blackwood

illustrations by Kerry Argent

Carolrhoda Books, Inc./Minneapolis

Millions of years before man or machine
lived Derek the dinosaur, little and green.

And all day long in his little stone house
he talked to his friend Montmorency the mouse.
And this is what he said . . .

"If only I looked like a *real* dinosaur
with a back full of scales and a mouth full of roar!

"Instead, Montmorency, what I like best
is sitting and knitting. (I've made you a vest.)

"Do you think I should try to be more like the others,
like Fang and like Fearless, my frightening brothers?"
Montmorency squeaked nervously, shaking his head.
"No. You're so much nicer than Fearless," he said.
"And knitting's so useful, and Fang makes me fearful!"
So Derek kept knitting, and felt much more cheerful.

And so the years passed, and Derek had knitted
a wardrobe of trousers and sweaters that fitted
his friend Montmorency, and dinosaur suits
for Fearless and Fang, and some warm woollen boots,
and mittens and tracksuits, and in a big box
there were hundreds of pairs of woolly blue socks.
You could hardly get into that little stone house
—there was just room for Derek, and space for a mouse.

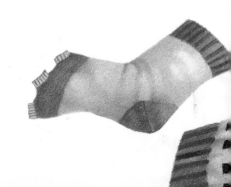

And still Derek sometimes
wished he could roar
and stamp up and down
like a real dinosaur.

But all of this time
in the wild outside
something was happening
slowly and strangely.

Slowly and strangely
something was happening
all those years
in the wild outside...

The world was becoming colder and colder;
the snow drifted down over cold hill and boulder.
All the fierce dinosaurs stamped up and down,
and their breath turned to ice on the cold stony ground.

Said Fearless to Fang (while coughing and wheezing)
"It's hard to be savage when you're nearly freezing!
I wonder how Derek is...let's go and see."
"I expect he is frozen," said Fang gloomily.

So...
those two scary dinosaurs (meekly and weakly)
went plodding and sneezing to Derek's front door,

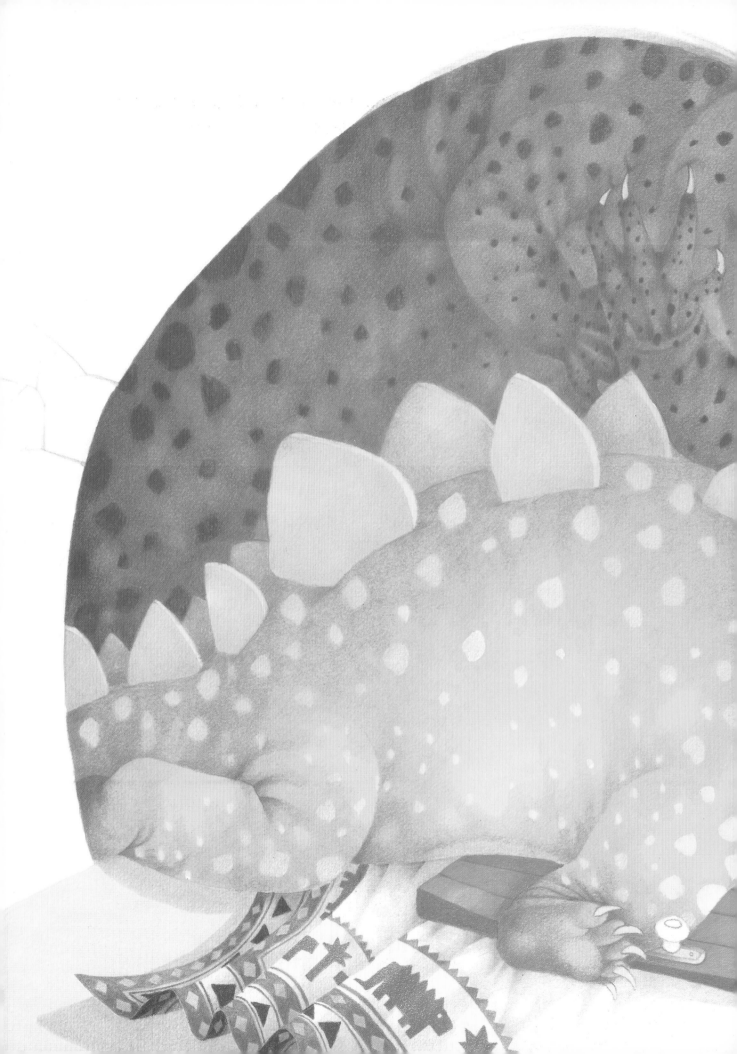

where they knocked with an effort (weakly and meekly)
and stumbled inside and collapsed on the floor.

Before Montmorency could say "one...two...three,"
little Derek had made them a nice cup of tea.

Before Montmorency could make up his mind
to come out from the chair he was hiding behind,
little Derek had measured them, found them some socks,

some mittens and trousers, and looked in his box
for sweaters and blankets and warm woolly things,
then joined six scarves together with woolly red strings.

And all you could see of Fang was his nose,

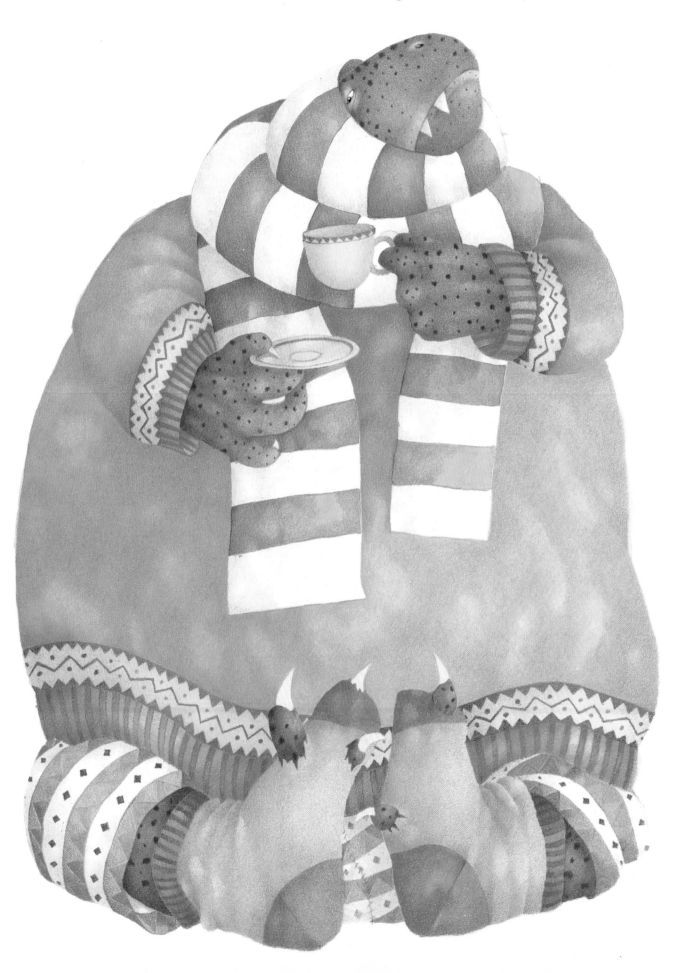

and Fearless was wrapped up right down to his toes.

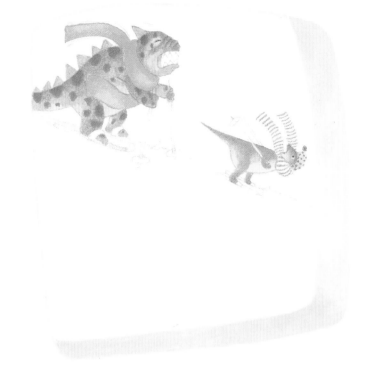

"I'm glad," remarked Fang
when he'd thawed out a bit,
"that dear little Derek
would rather just sit,
and go
    knittety
        knittety
            knittety
                knit!"

"And so am I," squeaked Montmorency.